In the beginning . . .

Martha was Helen's dog. She was an ordinary dog until . . .

. . . the day she ate alphabet soup.

The letters in the soup traveled up to her brain instead of down to her stomach.

That night Martha spoke:

When's dinner?

Steak is at the base of my food pyramid, along with alphabet soup. Above that is just meat in general.

Martha had a lot to tell her family.

Have you heard the one about the cat who walks into a pet shop and orders a can of dog food . . .

Martha just loved to talk.

Good dog, Skits!

Woof!

And talk . . .

Hello, world! I'm Martha and I'm talking to you!

Is the world ready for Martha?

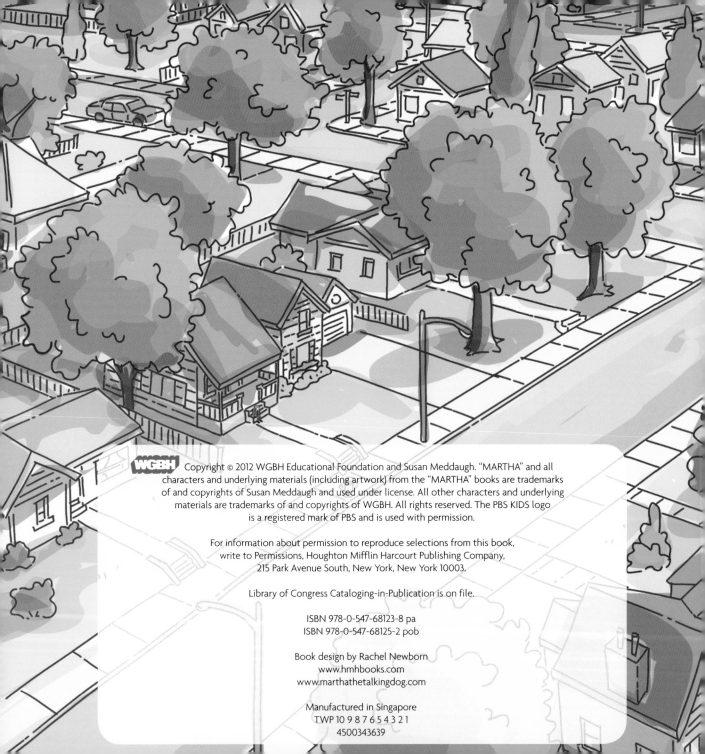

For information about permission to reproduce selections from this book, write to Permissions, Houghton Mifflin Harcourt Publishing Company, 215 Park Avenue South, New York, New York 10003.

Library of Congress Cataloging-in-Publication is on file.

ISBN 978-0-547-68123-8 pa
ISBN 978-0-547-68125-2 pob

Book design by Rachel Newborn
www.hmhbooks.com
www.marthathetalkingdog.com

Manufactured in Singapore
TWP 10 9 8 7 6 5 4 3 2 1
4500343639

MARTHA SPEAKS™

Purrfect Friends

Adaptation by Karen Barss
Based on the TV series teleplay written by Raye Lankford
Based on the characters created by Susan Meddaugh

Houghton Mifflin Harcourt
Boston • New York • 2012

Martha and Skits were napping when they heard voices in the backyard.

"Adorable!" Helen said.

"Isn't he? We just got him from the shelter," Alice said.

Martha perked up. "Shelter?! Come on, Skits! Let's go meet the new puppy!"

The two dogs ran outside.

"Hey, you guys," Helen said. "Come and meet your newest neighbor."

Alice smiled.

"We were hoping you could be buddies."

"Of course!" Martha said. "Any friend of yours is a friend of mine."

But Helen said, "Wait! Before I introduce you, promise you won't discriminate against him just because he's different from you?"

"Discriminate!" Martha exclaimed. "That means you aren't nice to folks because of how they look or where they're from. When have I ever done that?"

Helen and Alice exchanged a look and then stood up to reveal . . .

"CAT!" growled Martha. "GRRRRRRRoss!"

Helen scooped up the kitten.
"Martha, you promised!"
"Don't worry," Alice said. "He's only staying with us until he gets adopted."

Helen and Alice left with the kitten.

"There's different . . ." Martha said to Skits, "and then there's *cat!*"

Skits agreed. "WOOF!"

Martha went back inside to continue her nap.

Martha jumped up on her chair.

"YIKES!" she yelped. "This is my territory. Just because people think you're cute doesn't mean I like you."

But the kitten snuggled in close to Martha and started to purr.
As his eyes slowly closed, Martha had a surprising thought.

He is kind of cute.

She curled up around him.

Then Martha had another surprise. Skits walked into the living room.

He couldn't believe what he saw. *Martha* with the *kitten?*

Martha thought fast.

"How many times do I have to tell you?" she snapped at the kitten. "This is dog territory. Scram!"

Martha took the kitten outside.

She set the kitten gently down on the grass.

"Look, you're a nice kid," she said. "In a different world, maybe we could be buddies. But you're a cat and I'm a dog, and in this neighborhood I just can't socialize with you."

But the kitten nuzzled against Martha and purred.

Don't do that.

Then Martha whispered, "I guess we can be pals. It will be our little secret."

They played until it was time for the kitten to go home.

Late that night, when Martha thought Skits was sleeping, she snuck out of the house.

Below Alice's window, she called softly. "Kitten? Are you there?"

The kitten appeared at the window and climbed outside.

But just as they started to play, Skits appeared.
Martha could no longer pretend.
"Okay, okay!" she said. "I'm friends with a cat."

"You don't know anything about this kitten," Martha said.
"You're prejudiced."

Skits was offended.

"Yes, prejudiced," said Martha.

"It's when you decide you don't like someone before you even know him. Just give the kitten a chance."

Alice appeared at the window.

"I really like what you're saying about not being prejudiced," she said, "but could you save it until morning?"

"Sorry, Alice," Martha called. She turned to the kitten.

"Go to bed, little buddy," she said. "I'll see you in the morning."

The next morning, Martha couldn't wait to visit the kitten. "I'll be back for breakfast in a jiffy," she told Helen as she ran out the door. "I just want to say hello to my new friend."

When Martha got to Alice's house, Alice was waving as a car pulled out of her driveway.

"Bye!" she called. "Take good care of him!"

"What's going on?" Martha asked.

"The kitten got adopted," Alice replied.

"No!" cried Martha.
"Kitten! Stop!"
    She chased the car, but she couldn't catch it.

Back home, Martha was sad all day.
"I have something for you, Martha," said Helen.
It was a picture of the kitten.

"Oh, Helen! It looks just like him," Martha said.
"Would you like to visit him?" Helen asked. "His new family said you can come over anytime."
Martha was overjoyed.

Skits wanted to come too.

"We want to go now!" Martha said.

Skits howled in agreement.

"Aren't you worried about what the other dogs will say?" Helen asked.

"What do we care what a bunch of prejudiced mutts think?" Martha asked. "Nothing can come between us and our new friend."